MR. MEN
LITTLE MISS

The Christmas Contest

Roger Hargreaves

Original concept by
Roger Hargreaves

Written and illustrated by
Adam Hargreaves

The weeks before Christmas were a very busy time of year for Mr Tall. His phone did not stop ringing.

And who was calling Mr Tall?

All his friends who needed help hanging Christmas decorations on their houses.

Early each morning, Mr Tall set off across the countryside to the next house on his list.

Mr Bump was particularly grateful to see Mr Tall because Mr Bump and ladders were not a good mix!

There was no need for ladders when you had Mr Tall to help you put up your decorations.

Mr Tall went from house to house arranging coloured lights and decorations.

All kinds of Christmas decorations.

There were snowflakes.

And stars.

And snowmen.

And lights.

And lanterns.

And Santa's sleigh.

And ...

… bananas!

It could only be Mr Nonsense.

Well, at least the bananas matched
the Nonsenseland snow.

The only person Mr Tall couldn't help was Mr Messy.

His Christmas lights were in such a terrible, tangled-up, knotty mess that there was nothing Mr Tall could do with them.

Mr Tall's biggest job was at Little Miss Splendid's house.

She liked to have the very best display in the neighbourhood.

Well, what she really liked was to show off!

She had such a glittering display of lights that you could see them from space.

Father Christmas never had a problem finding her house on Christmas Eve!

"This year," said Little Miss Splendid, "we ought to organise a competition for the best Christmas house."

"I wonder why you suggested that?" smiled Mr Tall.

"It would be fun!" cried Little Miss Splendid.

"You should be the judge!" said Mr Tall.

"But then I couldn't enter," said Little Miss Splendid.

"I know," laughed Mr Tall, with a wink.

"OK, we'll both be judges, but next year I get to enter," said Little Miss Splendid.

And so the two of them organised the festive competition.

There were a lot of entries and Little Miss Splendid and Mr Tall were at the lighting up of each house.

Mr Perfect had high hopes.

But when he turned on his lights, nothing happened.

He couldn't understand what had gone wrong.

But what had gone wrong was Little Miss Naughty.

She had stolen all his light bulbs!

Little Miss Chatterbox's display only covered half her house.

Which Little Miss Splendid and Mr Tall thought was rather odd.

But not odd at all if you knew that the phone had rung halfway through Little Miss Chatterbox hanging up her lights.

And when had the phone rung?

Three days ago!

But her display was much better than Mr Mean's.

Little Miss Splendid and Mr Tall wondered why he had bothered.

Little Miss Scatterbrain had gone to a lot of trouble.

She had a wonderful display.

But it wasn't quite right.

Well, in fact, it was quite wrong!

Little Miss Splendid and Mr Tall visited a lot
of houses.

And some of the Christmas decorations were good,
but they couldn't find that extra special festive display
that they were looking for.

Something that would amaze them.

Something that would surprise them.

Finally, they arrived at Mr Messy's house.

They had very low expectations.

A tangled nest of wires hung limply on his roof.

Mr Messy turned on his lights.

And suddenly, that great big jumbled-up mess made sense, for it spelt out:

HAPPY CHRISTMAS.

Which was a huge surprise to Little Miss Splendid.

And it was a huge surprise to Mr Tall.

And it was a huge surprise to …

… Mr Messy!

"Well I never!" he exclaimed.

It was such an amazing surprise that Little Miss Splendid and Mr Tall declared him the winner on the spot.

"And next year you get to be the judge," said Little Miss Splendid to Mr Messy.

And then she grinned at Mr Tall.

Now, I wonder who will win next year's competition?